Karen's Nanny

**Other books by
Ann M. Martin**

P. S. Longer Letter Later
(written with Paula Danziger)
Leo the Magnificat
Rachel Parker, Kindergarten Show-off
Eleven Kids, One Summer
Ma and Pa Dracula
Yours Turly, Shirley
Ten Kids, No Pets
With You and Without You
Me and Katie (the Pest)
Stage Fright
Inside Out
Bummer Summer

For older readers:

Missing Since Monday
Just a Summer Romance
Slam Book

THE BABY-SITTERS CLUB series
THE BABY-SITTERS CLUB mysteries
THE KIDS IN MS. COLMAN'S CLASS series
BABY-SITTERS LITTLE SISTER series
(see inside book covers for a complete listing)

Karen's Nanny

The author gratefully acknowledges
Gabrielle Charbonnet
for her help
with this book.

Little Sister

Karen's Nanny
Ann M. Martin

Illustrations by Susan Crocca Tang

A
LITTLE APPLE
PAPERBACK

SCHOLASTIC INC.
New York Toronto London Auckland Sydney
Mexico City New Delhi Hong Kong

ISBN 0-590-50057-0

12 11 10 9 8 7 6 5 4 3   9/9 0 1 2 3 4/0

Printed in the U.S.A.   40
First Scholastic printing, January 1999

A Fresh Start

"Rabbit, rabbit," I whispered. I opened my eyes and sat up in bed. "Yes!" I said. "I remembered to say 'Rabbit, rabbit!'"

Why was I so excited about saying "Rabbit, rabbit"?

Well, if you say "Rabbit, rabbit" first thing in the morning on the first day of the month, you have good luck all month. And I had just said it not only on the first day of the month. I had said it on the first day of the whole year.

It was January first. New Year's Day.

1

I was sure I would have good luck for the whole year.

I peered out of my little-house bedroom window. (I will explain about my little house and my big house in a minute.) The ground was covered with beautiful, fresh new snow.

My good luck was starting already.

I leaped out of bed and ran to the kitchen. Mommy was at the table. So were Seth, who is my stepfather, and Andrew, who is my little brother. Andrew is four, going on five. I am seven.

"Good morning, Karen," said Mommy. "Biscuits or cereal for breakfast?"

"Cereal, please," I said. "Krispie Krunchies."

"I am sorry, Karen," said Mommy. "We are all out of Krispie Krunchies."

No Krispie Krunchies? Hmmph. My good luck had not lasted all year. It had not lasted even five minutes.

"We have Oatie-Os," Mommy suggested.

"Okay," I said. "I will have Oatie-Os. Thank you."

I was not going to let a little thing like no Krispie Krunchies upset me. It was a new year. There was new snow on the ground. The world was off to a fresh start, and so was I.

And the best way to make that fresh start last was to make a New Year's resolution. I had been thinking about it for days. But I had still not decided what my resolution would be.

Mommy had said a New Year's resolution should make you a better person. Hmmm. How could I become a better person? I was already pretty good. This was going to be hard.

Sometimes I forget to raise my hand in class. Sometimes I forget to use my indoor voice. So I could resolve always to raise my hand in class, and never to shout when I am inside.

No. Those things were not big enough.

A New Year's resolution should be about something big — something *important*. (Besides, I was not sure I could remember always to raise my hand and use an indoor voice.)

Maybe hearing my little-house family's resolutions would give me an idea for my own.

"Have you made a New Year's resolution, Seth?" I asked.

"I certainly have," said Seth. "My New Year's resolution is to get more exercise. I want to run in the Stoneybrook Ten-Kilometer road race in October."

"Gee," I said. That was a good resolution. But I did not think I could run that far. It was not the resolution for me. "What is your New Year's resolution, Andrew?"

"I am going to eat more cake and ice cream," said Andrew.

"Hmmm. O-kaay," I said. I was trying to be polite. But I did not think Andrew understood what New Year's resolutions are all about.

4

"What is your New Year's resolution, Mommy?" I asked.

"I have two resolutions," Mommy said. "While Seth exercises his body, I will exercise my mind. My first resolution is to read one play by William Shakespeare each month, for the whole year. January is *Romeo and Juliet*."

"Wow," I said. Mommy's first resolution was good too. But though I am an excellent reader, I was not sure I was ready for Shakespeare.

"What is your other resolution?" I asked her.

"My second resolution is even more important than the first. I resolve to find the perfect nanny for you and Andrew," she said.

Gulp. A nanny? Even though I was making a fresh, new start, that did not mean I needed a fresh, new person in my life.

2

Karen's Two Families

"Why do Andrew and I need a nanny?" I asked.

"Karen, you know that I am going to start working at the crafts center soon," said Mommy.

I nodded. It was true — Mommy had found a job making jewelry. She might even teach classes in jewelry-making.

"When I start work," Mommy continued, "we will need a nanny to take care of you and Andrew on the days you're here at the little house."

Oh, yes. I promised to explain about the little house, where Mommy and Seth live, and the big house, where my big-house family lives.

A long time ago, Andrew and I lived at the big house all the time, with Mommy and Daddy. Then Mommy and Daddy got divorced. Andrew and I moved with Mommy to the little house. Daddy stayed at the big house. (It is the house he grew up in.)

Then Mommy met Seth Engle, and they got married. That made Seth my stepfather, and his pets — Rocky, a cat, and Midgie, a dog — my steppets. The other little-house pets are my rat, Emily Junior, and Andrew's hermit crab, Bob.

Daddy also got married again, to a nice woman named Elizabeth Thomas. She had been married before too, and has four children of her own. David Michael is seven, like me. (He does not go to my school, Stoneybrook Academy. He goes to Stoneybrook Elementary.) Kristy is thirteen. She is gigundoly nice. Sam and Charlie are so old they go to high school. I also have a little sister named Emily Michelle. She is two and a half. Daddy and Elizabeth adopted her from a faraway country called Vietnam. And last there is Nannie, Elizabeth's mother, who came to live at the big house and help take care of all of us. Those are the big-house people. I have not even mentioned the pets yet! Shannon is David Michael's gigundo puppy; Scout is a Labrador puppy that Kristy is training to be a guide dog; Pumpkin is our brand-new black kitten; and Crystal Light the Second and Goldfishie are our sharks (just kidding!). Also, Emily Junior and Bob go back and forth when Andrew and I do. Andrew and I usually spend one month at the little house, and the next month at the big house. That way we can have time with both our families.

I made up special nicknames for my brother and me. I call us Andrew Two-Two and Karen Two-Two. (I got the idea from a book called *Jacob Two-Two Meets the Hooded Fang*.) Andrew and I are two-twos because we have two of so many things. We each have two mommies and two daddies, two houses, and two families. I have two bicycles, one at each house, and two stuffed cats who look exactly alike. Andrew and I have two sets of clothes, books, and toys. That way, we do not need to pack much when we go back and forth between our two houses. Also, I have two pairs of glasses — blue for reading, and pink for the rest of the time.

I even have two best friends. Hannie Papadakis lives across the street and one house down from the big house. Nancy Dawes lives next door to the little house. Hannie, Nancy, and I are all in Ms. Colman's second-grade class. We do everything together. We call ourselves the Three Musketeers.

Now I have something very, very sad to tell you. There used to be one other pet at the big house — Boo-Boo, Daddy's cat. Daddy had had Boo-Boo since before I was born. For a long time I did not like Boo-Boo very much. He was cranky. But as he grew old, he became nicer. Then he died. It was very tragic, especially for Daddy. I miss Boo-Boo a lot too. I wish he had not had to die.

Sometimes being a two-two is hard. Andrew and I miss the family we are not staying with. And changing houses is not always fun. Plus, a little while ago Mommy, Seth, and Andrew went to live in Chicago for several months. I went with them, but then I decided to come back to Stoneybrook and stay at the big house. Now everyone is back in Stoneybrook, and I am at the little house again.

The little-house family moved to Chicago. . . . Pumpkin came to live at the big house. . . . Boo-Boo died. . . . The little-house family came back. . . . And now there is going to be a nanny at the little house.

So many changes! I like excitement, but I was beginning to think I did not want so much change in my life. It seemed that as soon as I got used to things, they changed. It was exhausting.

Now Mommy said, "I have placed an ad in the *Stoneybrook News*. I will interview people who answer the ad. The ones I like will spend an afternoon with you. And you two will help me choose the perfect nanny. It will be just like finding our own Mary Poppins."

Maybe it would be. But I was not sure.

Project Jupiter

Two days later winter break was over and school started again.

Yippee! I love school. I was glad to be back. That is because I knew I would see Hannie and Nancy all day, every day. I would see the other kids in my class. And I would see Ms. Colman, my gigundoly nice teacher.

School is one thing that never changes. The Three Musketeers are always best friends. We always eat lunch together. We play at recess together. We even used to sit

13

next to each other in class, but now I sit in the first row with the other glasses-wearers, Ricky Torres and Natalie Springer, while Hannie and Nanny sit in the back. The Three Musketeers have a motto: "All for one, and one for all!"

At school, Pamela Harding is always my best enemy. (That is not really a good thing, but at least it never changes.) Jannie Morris and Leslie Gilbert are always Pamela's best friends.

Ricky is always my pretend husband. We got married on the playground one day.

Addie Sidney always zooms around in her wheelchair.

Terri and Tammy Barkan always look alike. (They are twins.)

Natalie's socks are always drooping.

And the other kids — Bobby Gianelli, Audrey Green, Omar Harris, Chris Lamar, Sara Ford, Hank Reubens, and Ian Johnson — are always themselves. They are very dependable that way.

And best of all, Ms. Colman is always, always, always gigundoly nice. She is the best teacher in the whole world. And she often has Special Announcements to make.

"Class," Ms. Colman said as we took our seats. "I have a Special Announcement to make." (See what I mean?)

"Hooray!" I shouted. Ms. Colman did not even remind me to use my indoor voice.

"We are going to start a new unit about the planets," Ms. Colman said. "As you all know, there are nine planets — Mercury, Venus, Earth, Mars, Jupiter, Saturn, Uranus, Neptune, and Pluto. And there are eighteen students in our class. If you all pair up with a partner, we will have nine pairs, one for each planet."

Ms. Colman is so smart. I had never realized that we had the perfect number of kids to study the planets.

"I have assigned each of you a planet partner," Ms. Colman continued. "Each pair of partners will draw a planet name out of a hat. That is the planet they will study. At the end of the unit, the planet partners will make a presentation about their planet to the class. And I will do a presentation on the sun."

Ms. Colman read out her planet partner list. I hoped Hannie or Nancy would be my partner. But Hannie was paired with Ian, and Nancy was paired with Ricky. (I decided not to be jealous that she was going to work with my pretend husband.)

Ms. Colman called out more pairs. At the end, there were only four names left: Addie, Bobby, Pamela, and me. I closed my eyes and wished hard that I would not be paired with Pamela.

"Karen and . . ." said Ms. Colman. I crossed my fingers. "Addie."

Yippee! I like Addie a lot. Plus she is smart. She would make an excellent planet partner.

Next Ms. Colman told the planet partners to pick slips of paper out of a hat. She used the purple knit cap with the green pom-pom she had worn to school. It is a very eye-catching hat.

16

When it was our turn, Addie and I reached in together. We chose a slip of paper. We unfolded it and read: JUPITER.

Jupiter! I knew all sorts of things about Jupiter. I rushed back to my desk and made a list of everything I knew about Jupiter:

1. Jupiter is the largest planet.
2. ?

Hmmm. Actually, I knew only one thing about Jupiter. But that was a start. I bet the partners who picked Uranus could not have named a single fact about it. (I could not have.)

"Now, planet partners," said Ms. Colman. "Please take ten minutes to meet and discuss your project."

Addie wheeled over to my desk. "This is going to be fun, Karen," she said. "I love planets. Jupiter is one of my favorites, because it is the biggest. And its Great Red Spot is so neat."

"Great Red Spot?" I asked.

"Yes," said Addie. "There is a giant hurricane constantly whirling around on Jupiter. From Earth, it looks like a big red circle. That is why it is called the Great Red Spot."

Gosh. Addie knew two things about Jupiter, and maybe more. I would have to work extra hard to keep up with her.

"Well," I said, clapping my hands. "I think we should get to work."

"Yes," said Addie. "It is time to launch Project Jupiter."

4

Best Behavior

That afternoon when I got home, Mommy had a snack ready for me — peanut butter on bread, and a glass of milk. I love peanut butter on bread.

Andrew was eating his snack already. He was down to the crust. He stood up from the table, put his cup and plate in the sink, and sat down again.

In between bites and gulps, I told Andrew and Mommy about Project Jupiter. I showed them my Project Jupiter notebook. I had

19

started a whole new notebook just for Project Jupiter.

Andrew had never even heard of Jupiter. He knew only Earth, Mars, and Saturn. Mommy had heard of Jupiter, of course. She even knew about the Great Red Spot.

"Project Jupiter sounds very interesting, Karen," said Mommy. "I am sure you and Addie will make fine planet partners."

I beamed. Mommy always knows what to say.

"Now, Karen, Andrew," Mommy said. Her voice sounded serious. "I have something important to discuss with you."

Andrew and I waited. I wondered what could be so important. Maybe it would be something important and fun, like a new swimming pool in the backyard.

"I have received quite a few responses to the nanny ad I placed in the *Stoneybrook News*," Mommy said. "I have picked three of the best people to interview."

Oh. We were not getting a swimming

pool in the backyard. We were getting a nanny.

I must have looked disappointed, because Mommy said, "Now, Karen, you know we talked about this just the other day."

"I know," I said. "I had not forgotten. I had been hoping you had forgotten."

Mommy smiled. "After I meet my three choices, they will each spend an afternoon with you two. Then we will decide together which of them we should offer the job to. Does that sound like a good plan?"

Andrew nodded. "We will pick the best nanny ever!"

"There's the spirit, Andrew," Mommy said. "And Karen?" She looked at me.

I nodded, but not very happily. I did not want a new nanny. I liked my little-house family just the way it was.

"Good," said Mommy. "Now you two run along. I have some phone calls to make. I must start setting up nanny interviews right away."

I stood up from the table and trudged out of the kitchen. I hoped Mommy noticed how sad I looked.

"Karen?" Mommy called after me.

"Yes, Mommy?" I answered sadly. Maybe she had changed her mind. Maybe I would not have to get used to a new nanny after all.

"Aren't you forgetting something?" she asked me.

Hmmm. Oh, yes. I had left my Project Jupiter notebook on the kitchen table.

"Oh, right," I said. I walked back into the kitchen, grabbed the notebook, and walked out again.

"Karen!" This time Mommy was not calling after me. This time she was calling *at* me.

"What?" I asked.

"You left your cup and plate on the table," said Mommy. "Please clear your place."

"Oh. Sorry. I forgot," I said, coming back into the kitchen. I gathered my cup and plate and placed them in the sink.

"Thank you," said Mommy. "And Karen? I am going to rely on you to be on your best behavior when the new nanny comes. She will be here to help you and Andrew, but I need you to help her too. You are not a baby anymore. You are seven years old, and I expect you to be responsible. I know you can be, if you want to be."

Mommy's voice was gentle, but I could tell she meant what she said.

"Do you understand?" Mommy asked.

"Yes, Mommy," I said.

"Good." Mommy smiled.

I tried to smile back at her, but I was not really able to.

Mommy wanted me to start acting more grown-up. But why should I have to change for the nanny — a stranger? I did not want a nanny at all. Would the nanny be on *her* best behavior? What if Andrew and I did not like any of the three choices? Would we have to put up with a nanny we hated?

I was used to my life the way it was. Now all of a sudden it was going to change.

Mommy would be at work. A strange nanny would be here in the afternoon when I got home from school. A nanny I had to be on my best behavior for. Why did I have to adjust myself to everyone else? It did not seem fair.

Well, I would try to be on my best behavior. I had promised Mommy.

But I did not feel cheerful about it.

5

Karen's Resolution

The next day was Friday. When I came home after school, I found Mommy in the kitchen talking to a young woman.

"Ah. Karen," said Mommy. "I would like you to meet Rose Wertzel. Rose is our first candidate for the nanny job. Rose, this is my daughter, Karen."

"Hi, Karen," said Rose. She gave me a big smile.

"How do you do?" I said politely.

Rose looked nice. But you cannot judge a

book by its cover. Maybe she was only nice around Mommy. We would see.

Mommy needed to talk with Rose some more, so she fixed me a snack and asked me to take it to my room to eat it. Usually I am not allowed to take food out of the kitchen.

I went upstairs to my room and closed the door. I put on my new Lemon Drops CD. The Lemon Drops are my favorite group. They are a little tart and a little sweet, just like their name. I danced around my room to the first song, "It's a Grrl's Wrrld." Then I sat at my desk to eat my snack.

I had my milk — ice cold, just the way I like it. I had my bread — whole wheat, my favorite. I had my peanut butter — crunchy, as usual.

But wait. What was this?

I held the bread up to the light of my desk lamp. The peanut butter looked suspiciously smooth. There were no little crunchies in it.

I took a bite. Smooth. Totally smooth.

Just to make sure, I took another bite. Smooth as silk.

First no Krispie Krunchies. I had had to eat Oatie-Os. Now what had happened to the crunchy peanut butter? Why smooth all of a sudden? We always ate crunchy at the little house. I could not remember a time, ever, when I was forced to eat smooth peanut butter.

I balled up my fist and banged it on my desk. Boo and crunchy bullfrogs!

I did not want smooth peanut butter! I wanted crunchy! It was what I was used to. I did not want to have to get used to smooth. What next? Would I get used to smooth, and then have to switch back to crunchy?

I had not liked it when the little-house family moved to Chicago. But I had gotten used to it. I had not liked it when Boo-Boo died. But I had gotten used to that. I did not like the idea of a new nanny. I knew I would have to get used to that too.

But this was the last straw. I did not want

29

to get used to a new style of peanut butter every day. I refused to. Enough was enough. I was tired of change. I would not change.

Suddenly I had a brilliant idea. I still had not made my New Year's resolution. This was it!

I resolved not to change, all year. In anything. I would put a stop to any and all changes in my life.

All at once I felt much better. I finished my snack. (Smooth tastes just as good as crunchy, actually.) I danced around the room to another Lemon Drops song, "Sister Strength."

With no changes, my life would be so much simpler. So much easier. So much better. I would know what to expect and when to expect it. I would be ready for everything that came my way. I would feel on top of things.

I was sure of it.

6

Start Not Changing Now

Over the weekend I worked out the details of my New Year's resolution. First I made a list of all the things that I could not possibly avoid changing:

Things I Cannot Help Changing
1. I will still change houses every month.
2. When summer comes, I will change from going to school to going to summer camp.
3. I will change my clothes every day.

4. When I want to read, I will change from my pink glasses to my blue glasses.
5. When I am done reading, I will change back to my pink glasses.

There. That just about covered it. I could not think of anything else I would have to change.

Next I started to think about all the things I would *not* change. There were lots. Many more than five.

I would do the same things every day. Every day would be exactly the same. No changes! This way, I would never forget to put things away, help clean up, and do my other chores.

Mommy would be so impressed at how grown-up I was becoming. I would be the most responsible person she had ever seen. I could tell my resolution was a good one, because it would help me become an even better person than I already was.

To help myself stay organized (I am an excellent organizer), I made up a schedule for myself:

My No-More-Changes Schedule
Monday – Friday
    7:00 – 8:00 — Wake up, get dressed, eat breakfast.
    8:00 – 8:30 — Go to school.
    8:30 – 3:00 — School.
    3:00 – 4:00 — Come home from school, eat snack.
    4:00 – 5:00 — Do homework and chores.
    5:00 – 6:00 — Play.
    6:00 – 7:00 — Eat dinner.
    7:00 – 8:00 — Take bath, read or watch TV, go to bed.
Saturday – Sunday
    8:00 – 9:00 — Wake up, get dressed, eat breakfast.
    9:00 – 12:00 — Play.
    12:00 – 1:00 — Eat lunch.
    1:00 – 6:00 — Play.
    6:00 – 7:00 — Eat dinner.

> 7:00 – 8:30 — Take bath, read or watch
> TV, go to bed.

Besides following a schedule, there were many other things I could do to avoid change. And I wanted to start not changing now. So I decided that, beginning Monday, I would do everything just the way I had done it last Friday. Luckily, Friday had been a pretty good day. I stopped to think . . . what *had* I done on Friday?

I had had orange juice and Oatie-Os for breakfast. So every day I would have O.J. and O.Os for breakfast.

At school I had lined up behind Bobby twice. So from now on, I would always line up behind him.

I had brought a bag lunch of a ham and cheese sandwich, an apple, and two cookies. Fine. Mommy would not mind fixing that every day. And I would not mind eating it. At home, I had eaten peanut butter (smooth!) on whole wheat bread for a snack. Then I had listened to the Lemon Drops and danced around my room. It sounded like a nice schedule. So every day, without fail, I would do all those things.

Let's see . . . how else could I not change?

I knew I would have to change my clothes every day (I am not a complete loony, you know). But if I chose all my clothes at the beginning of the week and wore whatever was on the top of the pile each day, it would almost be as if I were changing my clothes only once a week.

When Ms. Colman called on kids in class, I would raise my hand for every other question (it is polite to give the other kids a chance), no matter what. That way I, and everyone else, would know what to expect.

I had been reading a book called *The Adventures of Katie Kelleher*. As soon as I finished it, I would start it all over again. Fortunately, it was a terrific book.

Goodness. There were so many ways not to change: I would always wear my hair the same way. I would always brush my teeth the same way. I would make my bed the same way and arrange my stuffed animals the same way on the pillows. Plus I would do these things at the exact same time every day. I was going to be the most dependable person ever.

7

Rose Wertzel

On Monday morning at seven o'clock, I put my New Year's resolution into action. When my alarm went off, I leaped out of bed. I brushed my teeth, fixed my hair in a ponytail over to the side, and grabbed a shirt from one pile and some pants from the other pile. I had put seven tops in a pile, and seven bottoms in another pile, along with seven pairs of socks and seven undies. So every morning I just took whatever was on top of each pile, and zip, zip, zip — I was dressed!

I glanced in the mirror. I looked very nice in a white turtleneck sweater and some blue corduroys. The pair of socks on top of the pile had been blue, so that was perfect.

When I bounded into the kitchen, it was barely seven-thirty.

"Goodness, Karen," said Mommy, looking at the clock. "You are early this morning! And you look very nice."

I beamed as I dug into a bowl of Oatie-Os. I should have come up with this plan years ago.

At school I stuck to my resolution. I organized my schoolbooks inside my desk and resolved to keep them that way all the time. I hung my coat in my cubby as I always do.

At recess the Three Musketeers put on our coats and raced outside. I had decided that I would ask Hannie and Nancy always to play hopscotch first, then slide or swing, then jump rope, and then play four-square, if there was time. That way I would always know what to do at recess.

We played hopscotch. After hopscotch, I had a scheduled drink of water from the fountain. I checked my watch. Time for slide or swing.

"Let's go on the slide," said Nancy.

"Okay!" I agreed happily. At the slide, Bobby was already in line. Uh-oh. One of my rules was always to line up behind Bobby. So I ran ahead of Hannie and Nancy and zipped into line right behind him.

"Hey," said Hannie as they caught up with me. "If you want to go first, Karen, just say so." I could tell she was a little hurt that I had left them just to get in line. But it was too complicated to explain right now. I just had to be behind Bobby. I smiled and shrugged. Hannie and Nancy did not say anything else.

Later that day, I was practicing raising my hand for every other question. So far, I had known the answer to every question, although Ms. Colman had not called on me. Then she asked a question I did not know the answer to. But since it was a raised-hand question, I had to raise my hand. Guess what. Ms. Colman called on me.

"Um, I do not know," I admitted. I was embarrassed, but it was for a good cause.

Ms. Colman looked surprised, and called on Ian.

Mostly, as the week went on, my New Year's resolution made my life much, much easier. I remembered to clear my place after every meal. Since I did not have to pick out my clothes every morning, I was never late for breakfast. (I was never late anywhere anymore.) By Thursday I had finished *The Adventures of Katie Kelleher*. I could hardly wait to start reading it again.

Overall, things were going splendidly.

On Friday after school, the moment I came through the front door, I could tell something was baking in the oven.

"Mommy, Andrew!" I called, charging into the kitchen. "What smells so goo — "

That is when I noticed that they were not alone. Sitting at the kitchen table with them was Rose Wertzel, the nanny candidate I had met the other day.

"Oh," I said. "Hi, Rose."

"Hello, Karen," said Rose. She smiled.

"Karen, I am going upstairs to do some work," said Mommy. "Rose will spend some time with you and Andrew this afternoon."

Mommy left the kitchen. I sat down at the kitchen table.

"Rose made brownies," said Andrew happily.

"And I think they should be done just about now," Rose added. She stood up and took a pan of brownies out of the oven. They looked delicious. The kitchen was full of yummy brownie smell. There were whole walnut halves on top, just the way I like them.

"We need to let these cool for a few minutes," Rose said. "And then we can dig in."

I could not wait. My mouth was watering already.

But then I remembered. My after-school snack was always peanut butter on bread. Could I break my resolution just this once? No. I could not, I decided reluctantly. Not even for brownies.

"Um, I think I will have peanut butter on bread," I said sadly.

"What?" said Andrew. "Karen, there are *brownies*! Chocolate! With walnuts on top!"

"You do not like brownies, Karen?" Rose looked disappointed.

"Oh, no, I do. I love brownies," I said. "It is just . . ." My voice trailed off. "I am not in the mood for brownies right now."

"Oh, too bad," said Rose. "Well, it is no big deal. I just whipped up the brownies on the spur of the moment. You may have peanut butter instead, if that is what you want." She started slicing the brownies.

"It is what I want," I said miserably. I spread some peanut butter on a slice of bread. I watched Rose and Andrew eat their brownies.

"Mmmm, yummy!" said Andrew with his mouth full.

I felt like flinging my bread at him. But I did not. Flinging bread at Andrew was not part of my daily routine.

After our snack, Rose asked Andrew and me what we wanted to do.

"We could play Candy Land," said Andrew. "Okay, Karen?"

I looked at the clock on the stove. It was two minutes till four. Time for homework.

"I have to do my homework now," I said. I love playing Candy Land.

"Homework? On Friday afternoon?" said Rose. "How about playing with us, instead? If you do not want to play Candy Land, we could do something else."

"Like what?" asked Andrew.

"Oh, I do not know," said Rose thoughtfully. Then she grinned. "I like to be spontaneous. How about going in the backyard? I am sure we can find something fun to do."

"Okay!" said Andrew. He grabbed his coat and ran to the back door. "Come on, Karen!"

I glanced at the clock. Four o'clock.

"No," I said. "I have to do my homework now. It cannot wait."

"Well, okay, Karen, if you really must do your homework now," said Rose. "You are sure you cannot play?"

I really wanted to play in the backyard with Andrew and Rose. Rose seemed fun and nice. But I had to stick to my schedule.

"I am sure," I said. I trudged up the stairs to my room.

I put my homework on my desk. I could hear Andrew and Rose in the backyard, shouting and laughing. There was still snow on the ground from the week before. It sounded like Andrew and Rose were making snow angels.

I tried to do a math problem. I could not concentrate.

I love making snow angels.

I tried to read a chapter out of our social studies book.

It sounded like Andrew and Rose were making a snow fort now.

I kept reading the same sentence over and over.

I love making snow forts.

Now they were singing "Walking in a Winter Wonderland."

I love singing "Walking in a Winter Wonderland."

I hummed a little of it to myself. I could not read the sentence anymore. My eyes were too teary.

I sniffled. Rose would be the worst nanny ever. She did things on the spur of the moment. She liked being spontaneous.

Usually I am a big believer in being spontaneous. But I had a schedule now. And I knew I would never be able to keep my New Year's resolution if Rose were my nanny.

8

The Lemon Drops

At dinner Mommy asked Andrew and me how we liked Rose.

"She was wonderful, Mommy!" said Andrew. "We had fun in the snow, and her brownies were awesome."

"I am glad you liked her, Andrew," said Seth.

"Karen?" said Mommy. "What did you think of Rose?"

I gritted my teeth. "Umm," I said. "I was not crazy about her."

"Not crazy!" Andrew shouted. "Rose was perfect! She — "

"Andrew, indoor voice, please," said Mommy. She turned to me. "Now, Karen, tell us what you thought about Rose."

"She seemed nice enough, I guess," I admitted.

My family waited for me to say more.

"But she was too loud, too energetic . . . too, um, spontaneous," I said.

Mommy looked confused.

"Too loud? Too energetic?" Seth repeated. "Too spontaneous? For Karen Brewer? Is that even possible?"

"Um, well . . . yes, it is," I said.

Mommy and Seth looked at me in a funny way.

I thought about explaining my New Year's resolution to them. But Mommy, Seth, and Andrew had told me their resolutions. And so far Mommy had not read any Shakespeare, Seth had not gotten more exercise, and Andrew had eaten no cake. Resolutions seemed to work better when they were secret.

I had to come up with another reason for not liking Rose.

"I could not get my homework done, with all the noise," I said. I did not mention that the noise had come from outside and really had not been all that loud. Just fun-sounding.

"It was Friday afternoon," Andrew argued. "You did not have to do your homework then anyway. I want Rose."

"I do not," I said.

"Hmmm," said Seth. "I suppose it is important that Karen be able to do her homework when she wants to, even on a Friday afternoon," he added suspiciously.

"And we did agree that we would all choose the nanny together," said Mommy. "I am sorry, Andrew. For whatever reason" — she shot me a look — "Karen did not like Rose. We will have to hire someone else."

Andrew scowled at me.

I shrugged. "Maybe we will both like the next one," I said.

Andrew said nothing. He just kept scowling at me.

After dinner I went upstairs to my room.

Whew! I let out a sigh of relief. I had barely avoided a nanny disaster.

I looked at my schedule. I had given myself an hour every weekday to do homework. But I had forgotten to schedule any time on Saturday or Sunday for homework.

This afternoon, I had been so distracted that I had not gotten my homework for Monday done. And there was no room in my schedule to do it over the weekend. Oh, well. I would just have to catch up next week.

I put on the Lemon Drops, the way I did every day after dinner, and made myself dance around my room. It was not a very happy dance. I was getting a little tired of the Lemon Drops.

9

Springtime in January

"What a beautiful morning!" Mommy said as I walked into the kitchen on Monday. "The sun is shining, the snow has melted. It must be thirty degrees warmer outside!"

"I cannot believe it is January," Seth said cheerfully. "I hope this lasts."

I looked at what everyone was wearing. Instead of a heavy sweater and long pants, Mommy was in a corduroy dress. Seth was wearing a long-sleeved T-shirt. Andrew had on a turtleneck and jeans.

I had put on the top item on each pile of clothing I had laid out the night before: wool socks, an undershirt, heavy corduroy pants, a flannel shirt, and a wool sweater.

Uh-oh. I had a feeling I was wearing too many clothes.

"Blueberry muffin, Karen?" Mommy offered.

"Yes, plea — " I started to say. I love blueberry muffins. They are especially delicious with blueberry jam on them. I spotted the jar of jam on the table. The lid was already off the jar. The jam was calling to me. But my resolution said Oatie-Os every morning no matter what. I had to be strong.

"No thank you," I said. "I will have Oatie-Os."

Mommy cocked an eyebrow at me. "Okay," she said. "Or would you rather have Krispie Krunchies? I bought some more at the store."

Of course I would rather have Krispie Krunchies! I wanted to shout. But I did not. "Oatie-Os are fine."

52

"Karen has a new favorite," said Seth with a smile. I did not smile back.

Mommy handed Andrew a muffin and put a gigundoly huge dollop of jam on his plate.

"Karen, the paper says it is going to be quite warm out today," Seth said. "Maybe you should change into cooler clothes."

"Um, I think I will be okay," I said. I was already feeling too warm. But I could not change. "This way I will be ready if it turns cold later in the day."

"The forecast is for unusually warm weather all week, Karen," said Mommy.

Uh-oh again. Yesterday I had laid out a whole week's worth of heavy winter clothing. Hopefully the weather would change, since I could not.

"Choosing my own clothes is a big responsibility," I said. "And I am trying to be more responsible. I think I can handle dressing myself now." I smiled brightly at Mommy.

She opened her mouth to say something.

No sound came out. Then she smiled and asked Seth to pass the jam, please.

School was horrible. In my heavy winter clothing I was hot and uncomfortable all day long. There is nothing worse than sweating on the playground in January.

At lunchtime I was not quick enough to line up behind Bobby. Natalie was behind him. So I sort of butted in ahead of Natalie.

"Hey! No fair, Karen!" cried Natalie.

Hannie and Nancy looked at me and frowned from the end of the line. I wanted to explain, but I could not.

"No cutsies!" said Natalie. But I made myself face straight forward and stay behind Bobby. I felt as if my whole life depended on it.

"I'm going to tell Ms. Colman," said Omar Harris. He was right behind Natalie, so I had sort of cut in front of him too.

Ms. Colman was on lunch duty that day. Omar ran to her.

"Karen, you know it is not nice to cut into line," Ms. Colman said. "I am surprised at you. Everyone must wait their turn. Please go to the back."

I could not disobey Ms. Colman, resolution or no resolution. I slunk to the back of the line. Everyone frowned at me as I went past. I met Hannie's and Nancy's eyes. They did not look happy.

After lunch Ms. Colman told us to meet with our planet partners.

Addie showed me what she had done on Project Jupiter. She had taken excellent notes on an encyclopedia article. She had written them on index cards.

"The planet Jupiter is named for an ancient Roman god," Addie read from her notes. "In the Roman religion, Jupiter was king of the gods."

Gee. I had not known that.

"Okay, your turn," said Addie. "What did you find out about Jupiter?"

"Ummm . . ." I said. "Actually, I have not

had a chance to do any work on Project Jupiter." I did not mention that the reason I had not done any work was that my schedule did not allow for homework on weekends.

"Karen!" Addie said. Her eyebrows bunched up in the middle. "I am not going to do all the work for both of us, you know."

"I know," I said. For some reason my wool sweater was making me feel especially hot right then. "Do not worry. Everything is under control. I have a schedule all worked out. I will do my fair share of the work with plenty of time to spare."

"Well, okay," said Addie. "I guess."

Ms. Colman asked us to return to our seats.

I felt embarrassed. I am used to being a good student. Being embarrassed made me feel grumpy. On the way back to my desk, I bumped into Ricky. "Watch out!" I snapped at him.

"Watch out yourself," he said. "You big grouch."

I did not think that was a nice thing for a pretend husband to call his pretend wife. Even if it was true. I sat down at my desk, my face burning.

Boo and hot, sweaty bullfrogs!

10

Launch Delays

"Karen, would you come here, please?" called Mommy.

It was 4:01 in the afternoon. I was at my desk, in my room. I had just sat down to begin my homework. A library book about Jupiter lay open on the desk in front of me.

"Coming, Mommy," I called.

I found her in Andrew's bedroom.

"Would you please strip the sheets off all the beds, while I put a load of wash in?" Mommy asked me.

I hesitated. I really needed to do some

work on Project Jupiter. But Mommy needed my help. I had promised her that I was going to be more responsible. And the responsible thing was to help her with the housework.

My schedule said:

> 4:00 – 5:00 — Do homework and chores.

I guessed it would not break my resolution to help Mommy.

"Okay, Mommy," I said. "I would be happy to do the sheets."

"Thank you, Karen," said Mommy. "You are my special helper."

I smiled. I liked being Mommy's special helper. Besides, there would be plenty of time later in the week to work on Project Jupiter.

After I stripped the beds, Mommy asked me to help her put the clean sheets on them. Then I helped her fold laundry. Before I knew it, my scheduled homework hour was up. I was forced to play from five until six.

There went Monday.

On Tuesday I did not do any homework either. Mommy had to take Andrew to the mall to buy new shoes. Since we did not have a nanny yet, I had to go too. By the time we got back home, it was practically dinnertime. After dinner, I thought about skipping my bath and doing my homework instead. But I stuck to my schedule. I took a bath, read for awhile, then went to bed at eight o'clock sharp.

On Wednesday I helped Mommy set up her jewelry-making studio at the crafts center.

It was very interesting. Mommy showed Andrew and me how the solder gun (that is a tool shaped like a pistol with a very hot pointy tip) works. She uses the solder gun to melt the metal she makes into jewelry. We were not allowed to touch the solder gun.

After my bath that night, I wondered if I could read my book about Jupiter. Would that count as before-bed reading? I decided it probably did not. I picked up *The Adventures of Katie Kelleher*. I was on chapter three. Again.

On Thursday I had a dentist appointment. (No cavities, hooray!) I got home at 5:10. Boo and bullfrogs. When was I going to get this project done? I had been avoiding Addie all week, but sooner or later she would find out that I had not had a chance to catch up. She would probably be angry with me. She might tell Ms. Colman. And Ms. Colman had already spoken to me this week about cutting in line.

All of a sudden it was Friday. Even though I had meant to, I had not done my homework all week. Now it was the weekend, and I had no homework time in my schedule. What was I going to do? Project Jupiter was suffering from launch delays!

11

Trouble at School

Here is what I wore on Friday: red-and-green-plaid pants, a purple flowered sweatshirt, a magenta scrunchie, and blue-and-yellow polka-dot socks. I was not too hot. I was comfortable. But I felt like Bozo the Clown. And I looked like a fashion disaster. Somehow the piles of clothes I had laid out carefully on Sunday had not come out evenly matched.

Over breakfast I kept expecting Mommy to mention my outfit. I wished she would order me upstairs to put on clothes that matched. Then I would *have* to change.

But Mommy did not order me upstairs. She did not say a word about my clothes. She was respecting my choices. I wished she would not.

"Karen, is it circus day at school?" asked Andrew. He said this seriously.

"No," I replied. I did not say anything else.

I knew I looked ridiculous. But I could not change. I would have to go to school looking as if I had gotten dressed in the dark.

"Who can tell me what sight greeted turn-of-the-century immigrants when they first arrived in New York?" Ms. Colman asked.

I had no idea. We were supposed to have read a chapter on Ellis Island in our social studies book. I had not done any homework for more than a week. But I had not raised my hand for the last question (which I had not known either). So my resolution said I must raise my hand now.

"Please do not call on me," I begged silently. I kept my eyes on the floor and only raised my hand a little bit.

"Karen?" Ms. Colman called on me.

Aaugh! I thought hard. "Umm . . . the Empire State Building?" I guessed.

Ms. Colman frowned. "No, Karen," she said. "The Empire State Building was not built until the nineteen-thirties. Yes, Pamela?"

My best enemy was waving her hand as if she were being attacked by a swarm of flies. "The Statue of Liberty?" said Pamela.

"That is right. Very good, Pamela," said Ms. Colman.

Pamela smirked at me. I frowned back hard.

Ms. Colman asked another question. Luckily, I did not have to raise my hand for that one. I did not know the answer anyway.

Ian answered it.

"Did most of the immigrants speak English?" Ms. Colman asked next.

I timidly poked my hand in the air. "Yes,

Karen? Would you like another chance?" asked Ms. Colman. I wanted to cry.

I thought for a second. Probably, if people were moving to America for good, they would have learned English before they came, so they could get jobs right away.

"Um, yes?" I guessed.

Ms. Colman looked at me and shook her head. "No. Jannie?"

"No, Ms. Colman, they did not. Many could not read either — even simple things, like social studies homework." Jannie and Pamela smirked at each other, then at me. Ms. Colman did not see them.

It was the worst morning of my life. I raised my hand to answer every other question. Ms. Colman gave me a few more chances, but I didn't know any of the answers. After awhile, the class started giggling whenever I raised my hand. Then Ms. Colman ignored me. I felt terrible. Not only that, but every time I looked down at my outfit, I wanted to sink through the floor.

At lunch I found Hannie and Nancy sitting with Sara Ford and Audrey Green. I hesitated, then sat down with them. For a few minutes we ate silently.

"Karen, is there something wrong?" asked Hannie softly.

I wanted to blurt out that everything was wrong. I was dying to tell someone what was going on. But if I told the secret of my resolution, it would not work anymore. "No," I said. "Nothing is wrong. Why?"

"Well," Nancy said, glancing at Hannie. "You seem sort of . . . different lately."

"Yes," said Hannie. "You have changed."

What? I was bending over backward *not* to change! "I am not different!" I said. "I have not changed! I am exactly the same as I was yesterday, and the day before that, and the day before that!"

I slammed my milk down, splashing my flowered sweatshirt.

"You *have* changed, Karen Brewer," said Hannie firmly. She and Nancy stood up to leave. "You are not any fun!" They stalked out of the cafeteria.

I sat there, unhappy and angry, as Sara and Audrey looked at me curiously. So much for the Three Musketeers, I thought. I was not different. I had not changed. And I was still fun!

Back in class, Ms. Colman asked us to form our planet pairs.

"I borrowed a book from the library on Jupiter," said Addie, taking out her stack of index cards. The stack was thicker. She read from them: " 'Scientists are not sure if any part of Jupiter is solid. Some scientists think Jupiter might be a giant ball of gas.' "

Wow. A giant ball of gas. Who would have thought it?

"Okay, Karen," said Addie. "I am ready to find out what research you have done on Jupiter." She crossed her arms over her chest and looked at me.

Could this day get any worse? I did not think so. "Um . . . I have not exactly found out anything," I whispered, my head hanging down. "Yet."

"What?" Addie shouted. She jerked her wheelchair forward. It smacked into my desk with a loud *crack!* "You *still* have not done any work on our project?" I had never seen Addie so angry.

"Well, you see . . ." I wished I could explain things to Addie. I felt *soo* miserable. Then I saw something that made me feel even worse. Ms. Colman was heading toward us.

Uh-oh.

Karen Has Changed

"Hello, girls," said Ms. Colman, smiling. "You two are working on Jupiter, right? How is it coming along?"

I waited for Addie to tell Ms. Colman what a bad planet partner I had been. But she did not.

"Um, it is coming along okay," Addie said. She showed Ms. Colman the work she had done.

"That is very good, Addie," said Ms. Colman. "But all these notes are in your handwriting. Karen, where are your notes?"

71

Addie quickly answered for me. "Well, you see, Ms. Colman, Karen and I decided that I would take all the notes, because my handwriting is neater, and . . ." Addie rambled on.

I realized that even though I had been a terrible planet partner, Addie did not want me to get in trouble. She was covering for me.

But, I thought, if Ms. Colman figured out the truth, then Addie might get in trouble for trying to fool her. And Ms. Colman was looking at Addie as if she did not believe a word Addie was saying. I felt bad enough without getting Addie in trouble too.

"I have not done any work on Project Jupiter," I blurted out.

"Is this true, Addie?" Ms. Colman asked.

Addie nodded silently.

"Addie should not get in trouble," I said. "She was only trying to — "

"Addie is not in trouble, Karen," said Ms. Colman. She looked unhappy. "But I would like to see you after class today."

Now it was my turn to nod silently.

* * *

"Karen, I am becoming concerned about you," Ms. Colman said.

It was after class. All the other kids had left the classroom. It was weird to be in room 2B when it was so quiet. I could hear the *squeak, squeak* of Hootie, our guinea pig, running in his exercise wheel. I hoped I would not miss my bus.

"You are usually one of my best students," Ms. Colman said. "But lately you have not been yourself. You have been cutting into line and upsetting your classmates."

I thought about the Bobby rule and hung my head.

"You obviously have not been doing your homework," continued Ms. Colman. "You have not been able to answer a single question all week. Yet you keep raising your hand. You have been slowing down the whole class."

I hung my head lower.

"And now, today, I learn that you have not

done any work on your project with Addie. Karen, it is not fair for you to let Addie do all the work. I am sure Addie is disappointed in you, and I must say I am too."

I was not sure I could hang my head any lower, but I tried. I felt hot tears well up in my eyes.

"Now, Karen, look at me," said Ms. Colman.

I raised my eyes. There was Ms. Colman's kind and gentle face.

"It seems as if lately you have not been the same old Karen Brewer," she said. "You are different somehow. You have changed."

What? First Hannie and Nancy, and now Ms. Colman! They had all said that I was different. That I had changed.

Why did people keep saying that? I was not different. I had not changed at all!

"Maybe you are just going through a rough patch," said Ms. Colman. "Everyone does, now and then. But I would like to talk to your parents, to let them know what has been happening at school. I think they would want to know. Do you agree?"

"Yes, Ms. Colman," I whispered, so my voice would not crack.

"Good," said Ms. Colman. "Now run along. You do not want to miss your bus."

The Second Candidate

"**K**aren, this is Mrs. Hamilton," said Mommy as I walked into the kitchen. "Mrs. Hamilton is here to see about the nanny position. Mrs. Hamilton, this is my daughter, Karen."

I shook Mrs. Hamilton's hand.

"Nice to meet you," I said. I did not really mean it, but it was the polite thing to say. Mrs. Hamilton had bony fingers and a strong grip.

Mommy told Andrew and me that she would be out in the backyard for a while.

Mrs. Hamilton would fix us a snack.

"I would like a bagel with cream cheese," said Andrew.

"Peanut butter on bread for me, please," I added.

Mrs. Hamilton shook her head. "Cream cheese? Peanut butter? Too heavy. Top of the food pyramid!" she said. "I will see what is in the refrigerator."

While Mrs. Hamilton poked around in the fridge, I looked at Andrew. His eyes were wide. He shook his head hard.

I knew what Andrew was saying. He was giving the idea of Mrs. Hamilton as our nanny a big *"No!"*

"Here is the ticket!" Mrs. Hamilton exclaimed. She started chopping something on the counter. Then she turned and put a plate before Andrew and me.

On the plate were carrot and celery sticks.

"Eat up, children!" said Mrs. Hamilton. She crunched a carrot stick. "Mmm! Delicious!"

"Yuck!" said Andrew. "Bleh!"

Mrs. Hamilton frowned. "That is not very polite, Andrew. Carrots and celery are delicious and healthful. But if you are not hungry, you do not have to eat them."

Andrew stuck out his lower lip. "I do not want any snack," he said.

My chin jutted out. "I do not want one either."

"Fine," said Mrs. Hamilton. "Then I am sure you will eat a good dinner." She put the plate away. I felt very hungry.

"And now it is time for you to do your homework," said Mrs. Hamilton. "I shall read to Andrew in the living room. I have a nice book of moral lessons."

Andrew looked unhappy.

I glanced at the kitchen clock. It was only 3:20.

"It is not my homework time yet," I said. "I do not start my homework until four. And besides, today is Friday. I do not have to do my homework until Sunday." (I did not mention that my schedule did not allow for homework on Sunday.)

"Why wait until four?" asked Mrs. Hamilton. "If you begin now, you will be finished sooner. Then you can relax all weekend. So hop to it!" She gave me a toothy smile. "Come along, Andrew."

I took my social studies book out of my backpack. I turned to the chapter I should have read earlier in the week. It was all about Ellis Island. There was a picture of the Statue of Liberty (not the Empire State Building).

My goodness, was Mrs. Hamilton ever no-nonsense! Having her for a nanny would be like being in the army. I could tell she believed in rules, rules, rules. There was no way I would ever want . . .

Hmmm. Wait a second. Mrs. Hamilton was very firm, it was true. But so was my schedule. Mrs. Hamilton seemed like the kind of person who would appreciate someone like me, who lived on a strict schedule. If I explained to her how my schedule worked . . .

Ring, ring.

I heard Mrs. Hamilton pick up the telephone in the living room.

"Mrs. Engle is not available right now," she said. "I see. Karen's teacher. I will tell Mrs. Engle you called, Ms. Colman."

Mrs. Hamilton poked her head around into the kitchen. "That was your teacher, Karen. It seems she wishes to speak with your mother."

Mrs. Hamilton gave me a meaningful look, and I knew what the meaning was: *I bet you need to straighten up at school.*

14

Wonders Never Cease

"I hated her," said Andrew. "She was awful. She was terrible. She was the worst."

Seth passed me the mashed potatoes, and I plopped a big mound on my plate. We were eating dinner and talking about Mrs. Hamilton.

"Well, I guess we know how Andrew feels about Mrs. Hamilton," he said. "Karen? How do you feel?"

"Hmm," I said thoughtfully. Mrs. Hamilton had been kind of yucky. On the other hand, I still thought she was someone who might be open to the idea of my schedule. "I did not think she was so bad."

"What?" Andrew almost fell out of his chair. "She was like Cruella DeVil, Ursula the Sea Witch, and the Wicked Witch of the West all rolled into one! Only meaner!"

"She was not that mean," I said. "Okay, she was a little strict. But that is not necessarily a bad thing."

"I will remember you said that next time you break a house rule," Mommy said, smiling. "But seriously, Karen, you actually liked her?" I could tell that Mommy was surprised.

"Maybe 'like' is a bit strong," I admitted. "But I did not hate her."

Mommy shook her head. "Will wonders never cease?" she muttered. "Karen, you amaze me sometimes. I was certain you would say you did not like Mrs. Hamilton. You and she did not seem to get along. She said you were a — how did she put it? — 'a headstrong, obstinate child.'"

I shrugged. Whatever that meant.

"I think perhaps Mrs. Hamilton would be happier nannying other children," Seth observed. "For her own good, we should not offer her the job."

"Great," said Andrew. "Thank you!"

"Hmph," I said.

"I agree, Seth," said Mommy. "Since Andrew did not like Mrs. Hamilton, she is not the nanny for us. Remember, we must *all* agree on a nanny. We will have to keep looking."

"Maybe the next candidate will be the one," said Seth.

"I hope so," said Mommy. She turned to Andrew and me. "I was sure you two would agree on a nanny. But Andrew liked Rose and Karen did not. And Karen liked Mrs. Hamilton and Andrew did not. I am wondering whether we will be able to find a nanny who will please everyone."

I felt bad for Mommy. One of her New Year's resolutions was to find us the perfect nanny. Now she was beginning to doubt whether that was possible.

Soon dinner was over. Seth started to clear the table, and I offered to help him.

"Why, thank you, Karen," said Seth.

"Mrs. Hamilton told me that Ms. Colman called this afternoon," said Mommy. "I think I will return her call now. Do you know what she wanted, Karen?"

"Um," I muttered.

"Probably to tell you about some PTA meeting or something," said Seth.

"Um," I said again. Uh-oh. I did not want to be around when Mommy talked to Ms. Colman.

I checked the time. Five minutes to seven. Close enough.

"Seth, I just remembered I have something very important I have to do in my room right now," I said. "Sorry. I will help you some other time."

I ran to my room as quickly as I could and closed the door behind me. I put the Lemon Drops on the CD player, as I did every evening at seven o'clock.

The first, annoying notes of "It's a Grrl's

Wrrld" filled the room. I gritted my teeth. I could not bring myself to dance around my room.

I had listened to the Lemon Drops every single day, and I had grown to hate them.

15

Karen's Confession

The Lemon Drops were singing "2gether 4ever" (that is the way it is spelled) when I heard a knock on my door.

"Karen?" Mommy called. "May I come in?"

"Yes, Mommy," I said.

Mommy sat on my bed.

I turned off the Lemon Drops and sat next to her with my hands folded in my lap. I could not look at her.

"I spoke to Ms. Colman," Mommy said gently. "She is concerned about you. She said you have not been yourself at school lately. She said you have been disruptive. That you do not seem to know what is going on in class. And that you have not been doing your homework. Is this true, Karen?"

It was true. Suddenly, I realized that Ms. Colman and Hannie and Nancy were right. I *had* changed — and not for the better. Because of my resolution not to change, everything was a mess. My life had become a disaster.

I tried to say, "Yes, Mommy," but I could not. I felt as if a huge ball of sticky gum were in my throat. My eyes were watering, and my glasses were beginning to mist up.

Finally I nodded my head yes, and a tear slid down my nose. It hung on the tip, and then fell onto my hand.

That did it. I burst into tears and buried my head in Mommy's side. (I know it was a little babyish, but I was very upset.)

"Okay," said Mommy. She stroked my hair. "It is okay."

I sobbed for awhile. It felt as if I had been

holding the tears in for a long time. Crying was a great relief.

"Please tell me what has been going on," Mommy whispered.

I nodded and wiped away my tears. I was dying to tell someone. I could not tell Hannie or Nancy. I could not tell Ms. Colman. But I have always been able to tell Mommy everything.

"Do you remember how we all made New Year's resolutions?" I began.

"Yes, I remember," said Mommy. "Seth resolved to get more exercise. Andrew resolved to eat more cake and ice cream. And I resolved to find us a nanny and read Shakespeare."

"Right," I said. "And I noticed that none of your resolutions seemed to be working. So I decided to keep mine secret."

"And what was your resolution?" Mommy asked.

"Well, everything kept changing," I said. "I went to Chicago, then I came back. You and Seth and Andrew stayed there for awhile. Then you came back too. I was at the big house for months and months. Now I am at the little house again. The big house got a new cat, and then Boo-Boo died. I found out I was getting a nanny at the little house. It was too much change. Everything kept changing! So I resolved not to change in any way. To keep everything the same as much as possible."

There. Now Mommy knew how all my problems began. I waited for her to tell me she understood.

"I am afraid I do not understand, Karen," said Mommy. "What does this have to do with your trouble at school?"

So I explained how I had set up a schedule for myself. I showed her the schedule. (She seemed very impressed.)

I told her about how I laid out my clothes at the beginning of each week, and how I always wore my hair the same way, and how I always ate the exact same breakfast in the morning, lunch at noon, and snack in the afternoon. Mommy nodded thoughtfully.

I told her about always lining up behind Bobby, and about raising my hand for every other question. I explained how, even though I tried, I had not been able to do any homework in weeks.

I told Mommy about how I had thought that not changing would make me more responsible. But I had ended up being less responsible than ever.

It took a long time to explain. Who would have thought that one little resolution could get so complicated?

"And the worst part," I finished, "is that I cannot change back to the way I used to be. My resolution was to not change at all! I am stuck this way! Forever!" I burst into tears again.

16

The New New Year's Resolution

"I think I know now why you did not like Rose and did like Mrs. Hamilton," said Mommy. "Having Rose around would have made sticking to a schedule difficult, right?"

I nodded.

"And Mrs. Hamilton would have liked the idea of a strict schedule," Mommy said. "Right?"

I nodded again.

"Oh, Karen," said Mommy. She hugged

me close. It felt great. "I understand how you feel — about too much change in your life. Sometimes I feel the same way."

"You do?" I asked. Gee. It never occurred to me that Mommy might feel that way also.

"Yes, I do," said Mommy. "And I have not been looking forward to the changes the new nanny will bring in all of our lives. I really like taking care of you and Andrew myself. I like us to have a lot of time together. And I do not really like the idea that I have to share you with a stranger. But although it will be difficult, in the end, I think it is the best thing for us as a family. I will be very happy working at my new job. And we will have a little more money, which will make things easier. But I cannot feel good about having a nanny unless you and Andrew are happy and comfortable with her. That is why it is especially important to me to find the perfect nanny."

"I understand," I said. "I would like to have the perfect nanny too."

"I have an idea," said Mommy. "Maybe it

is not too late to change your New Year's resolution. After all, it is still January."

"Yes, but I told you, I resolved not to change," I reminded her. "Changing my New Year's resolution would be the biggest change of all."

"Maybe not," said Mommy. "Look at it this way: If you change your resolution about not changing, that breaks your resolution only once. If you stick with your resolution about not changing, every little change you make will break your resolution."

"Hmmm," I said. "You have a point." I thought about it some more. The more I thought about it, the more it seemed like a good idea. I had to do something. "Okay," I said. "I will change my resolution to something new. But what should it be?"

"I suggest you help me with my resolution," said Mommy.

"But I am too young for Shakespeare!" I exclaimed.

Mommy laughed. "No, silly," she said. "I want you to resolve to help find the family the best nanny ever. Do you think you can do that?"

I tapped my finger against my chin. "Yes, I guess so," I said. "That will be my new New Year's resolution. I will help find us a Mary Poppins of our own."

"Great," said Mommy, hugging me. "You know, not all change is bad, Karen. We need a little change every now and then, to keep us fresh."

"I know," I said. I hugged her back. "Just not all the time."

"Right," said Mommy. She stood up. "Well, I am glad we have solved this problem. And I hope things will get back to normal at school."

"They will," I said.

"Good," said Mommy as she went out the door.

Mommy was right. A little change was good. I knew that. I could see that I had gone overboard, trying to stop *all* change. From now on I would try to deal with changes as they came.

96

Except for one thing.

For some reason, I still did not want to have to get used to a new style of peanut butter ever again. Going from crunchy to smooth was what had started this whole thing. Now that I was used to smooth, there was no way I was going back. It was smooth or nothing.

I promised myself that.

Many Apologies

Monday was a big day for me. It was also a very good day.

For the first time in weeks, my clothes were perfect for the weather. Plus, they matched. I wore black leggings and my yellow taxi sweater. I pulled my hair back in the center, not on the side, and wore a matching yellow scrunchie. I felt great!

On the playground before class, I found Hannie and Nancy. They were playing hopscotch. I waited till Hannie had finished hopping to eight and back. Then I said,

"I am sorry I have not been much fun lately."

Hannie and Nancy glanced at each other. Nancy said, "We do not understand what is going on. You have been cutting in line. You have been grumpy. And you looked so . . . strange. What is happening with you?"

I told them about my first New Year's resolution. I explained how, instead of making my life better, it only made it harder. And when my life is hard, I am hard to be around.

"But I decided to change my resolution," I said.

"Thank goodness!" said Hannie and Nancy. They both gave me big hugs. I hugged them back.

We were the Three Musketeers again! All for one and one for all!

Next I found Addie. She was playing wall-ball with Ian. Wall-ball is a cross between Ping-Pong and baseball. Addie is very good at it. (She was beating Ian, seventeen to six.)

"Ian, may I speak with Addie alone for

a minute?" I asked him. (I sounded very grown-up and important.)

"Um, sure," said Ian. He practiced tossing the ball against the wall while Addie rolled her chair after me.

"What do you want, Karen?" Addie asked. I could tell she was still mad at me.

"I want to apologize," I said. "I have been a lousy planet partner. But I will make it up to you." I did not think Addie needed to know about the New Year's resolution, so I did not tell her. "Last night I read three chapters of a book about Jupiter. I took notes. I have been thinking about our report."

"Really?" asked Addie. "It is due on Friday. Do you think we will be able to finish it?"

"Absolutely," I said. "You will see. I will work hard on Project Jupiter. I promise."

Addie nodded. "Okay," she said. "Now I have to get back to my game." She whispered to me, "Four more points and I will have beaten Ian five times in a row."

I giggled. "You go, girl."

Next I found Bobby. He, Hank, Ricky, the Barkan twins, and Sara were playing tag. Bobby was not happy when I dragged him away from the game.

"What is it?" he demanded.

"I am sorry," I said.

"For what?" Bobby asked.

"I am sorry for cutting in line behind you all the time for the last two weeks." I knew that I should really apologize to all the kids I had cut in front of. But that was too complicated. Apologizing to Bobby would have to cover it.

"What are you talking about?" Bobby said. He looked at me as if he thought I were a loony.

"Never mind," I said. "Just tell me you accept my apology."

"Fine," he said. "Okay. Can I go back to my game now?"

I nodded. Bobby ran back to the tag game, shaking his head.

Three down, one to go. But the last one

would be the hardest of all. I went inside to our classroom. Ms. Colman was at her desk, looking at some papers.

"Ms. Colman?" I said.

"Karen," said Ms. Colman. "Come in. What can I do for you?"

I stepped into the classroom. "I wanted to say I was sorry," I said. "I did not mean to cause problems in class, or to let Addie down. But that is what happened, and I am sorry it did. I will not let it happen again."

Ms. Colman smiled. "I believe you will not," she said. "I am glad you are your old self again. I missed you."

"Thank you. I am glad too," I said. And I meant it.

Two Projects

Now that I did not have a schedule telling me what to do at every moment of the day, I was able to tackle Project Jupiter.

After school Mommy drove me to the library. I checked out three more books on the planets.

All afternoon I read Jupiter books. There was a lot of interesting information in them. For instance, Jupiter is 88,640 miles around its middle. (Earth is only 7,920 miles around.) I had not known that before.

After dinner Seth helped me surf the

Internet. Just before bedtime we found NASA's Web site. I did not have time to look through it, but I wrote down the URL (that is the Internet address). I would come back to it later.

Project Jupiter had finally taken off!

The next day I went to work on Project Nanny. I wanted to help Mommy find the best nanny ever. I had found such good information about Jupiter on the Internet, I thought I would try it for nannies too.

Boy, was I disappointed. Seth helped me search and search for a Web site listing perfect nannies, but I could not find anything.

Then Mommy suggested I try the library and the video store.

"Why?" I asked. "Do you think there will be a list of nannies there?"

"No," she said. "But you could read *Mary Poppins* and get ideas from it. And we could rent the movie version of *Mary Poppins*. It was one of my favorites when I was your age."

I checked *Mary Poppins* out of the library and started reading it to Andrew. (I am an excellent reader-alouder.) It was very funny. Andrew and I loved it.

We also rented *Mary Poppins*. The lady from *The Sound of Music* was in it (I had seen that on TV once). The boy and girl in *Mary Poppins* reminded Andrew and me of ourselves. They needed the perfect nanny, just like we did. *Mary Poppins* got four thumbs-up from Andrew and me.

Meanwhile, all week I was reading my books on Jupiter. I went back to NASA's Web site and found out a whole lot more about Jupiter.

Did you know that Jupiter has rings? They are not as big as Saturn's, but they are there. I printed out a photograph from the NASA Web site to prove it. I also printed out a bunch of other photographs. Addie was going to be very pleased with the visual aids I was collecting.

On Thursday afternoon Andrew and I finished reading *Mary Poppins*. Mommy had returned the video that morning (we had watched it twice).

Andrew and I made a list. In order to be just like Mary Poppins, the perfect nanny would have to:

- be very nice
- sing sweetly
- play games (all sorts)
- never smell of barley water (whatever that is)
- carry an umbrella
- be friends with a chimney sweep
- be able to fly.

(We knew she would not really be able to fly, but we put it in anyway.)

If our nanny was all of those things — or even most of them — then we would have found a Mary Poppins of our very own. And I was sure we were going to.

19

Third Time a Charm

On Friday morning Addie and I made our presentation. It went great. We took turns talking about Jupiter. I showed the photographs I had printed out from the NASA Web site. Addie brought a papier-mâché model of Jupiter, with the Great Red Spot painted on. It was very realistic.

The kids clapped when we were done. And Ms. Colman gave me a special smile. I knew she was glad that I really was my old self again.

After we went back to our seats, Addie

said, "You sure came through in the end, Karen."

"You did too, Addie," I said. "Of course, you came through in the beginning too."

Addie and I laughed.

"I'm ho-ome!" I sang out, coming into the kitchen.

Mommy and Andrew said hello.

"Where is the nanny?" I asked. "I thought she was supposed to be here already."

"Her plane was delayed by the weather," said Mommy. (It had been raining all day.) "She should be here any — "

Dingdong. The front doorbell rang.

"I will get it!" Andrew and I shouted at the same time. We raced to the front door and swung it open.

"Hello," said the woman standing on the welcome mat. "My name is Merry Perkins. I have just flown in from Miami." She hooked an umbrella over her arm and stuck out her hand. "You must be Karen and Andrew."

Her name was Merry Perkins? That

sounded almost exactly like Mary Poppins!

She said she had just *flown* in!

She was carrying an umbrella!

Andrew and I looked at each other in astonishment as we took turns shaking her hand.

Mommy came into the foyer and met Merry Perkins too. (They had already talked on the phone a bunch of times.) Then Mommy went upstairs, so we could have time alone with Merry.

We had a million questions for her.

"Can you sing?" "Are you nice?" "What does barley water smell like?" "Do you know any chimney sweeps?" Andrew and I asked her.

Merry Perkins laughed (she had a very nice laugh) and tried to answer our questions.

"Yes, of course I can sing," she said. "Everyone can sing. Some people sing better than others, though." Then she sang a little of the song about "Doe, a deer, a female deer." Merry was one of the people who could sing well.

"My friends think I am nice," she said. "I do not know what barley water smells like. And I do not know any chimney sweeps."

Hmm. No chimney-sweep friends. Still, Merry Perkins seemed just about perfect anyway.

Then she suggested that we make peanut-butter cookies.

"Oh, boy!" said Andrew as we followed Merry into the kitchen.

"Let's see," said Merry. "I know a special recipe for the world's best peanut-butter cookies." She rustled around in the cupboards, taking out ingredients.

"We will need a spoonful of sugar. . . ." she said to herself.

I looked at Andrew. He looked at me. His eyes were wide open in amazement. "A spoonful of sugar!" he mouthed at me.

"I know!" I mouthed back.

Merry Perkins was too good to be true.

". . . and a cup of crunchy peanut butter," she finished.

Crunchy? Oh, no! Not crunchy. Merry Perkins would be perfect, if only she would not insist on crunchy peanut butter. It was the one thing I refused to change!

I would hate to have to turn away the perfect nanny because she liked the wrong kind of peanut butter.

Merry rooted through the cabinets, looking for crunchy peanut butter.

At last she turned to us. "Oh, well," she said, holding up the jar of smooth. "Smooth is just as good. We can throw in some chocolate chips for oomph."

Hooray! Merry did not insist on crunchy.

She was the perfect nanny.

20

Merry Perkins It Is

"And what did you think of Merry Perkins?" Mommy asked Andrew and me over dinner.

"I loved her!" Andrew exclaimed. "She is the best!"

Mommy smiled. "I am glad to hear she met with your approval, Andrew. Karen, what did you think?"

I decided to tease Andrew a little.

"Ummm . . ." I said, as if I were thinking it over.

"Karen!" Andrew wailed. "I cannot believe that you do not — "

"I thought Merry Perkins was wonderful," I said, laughing. "Even though she does not know any chimney sweeps."

Andrew heaved a big sigh of relief.

"I liked her a lot too," said Mommy. "And what is more, Merry makes pottery. She sells her pottery and also gives lessons. That means she has a very flexible schedule. It is no problem for her to work one month on and one month off, as you two go back and forth between houses."

"Then is it decided?" Seth asked.

"Yes!" Andrew shouted.

"Yes!" I shouted.

"Merry Perkins it is," said Mommy. "She will be our very own Mary Poppins."

After dinner I went to my room. I put the Lemon Drops in the CD player. Now that I did not have to listen to them every day, I liked them again.

I thought about how I liked the Lemon Drops, then hated them, then liked them again. It is funny how feelings can change — and even change back sometimes.

My first New Year's resolution had been a mistake. Sometimes change is okay. Of course, you have to draw the line somewhere, and I had drawn mine in peanut butter.

My second New Year's resolution had worked out much better. I had helped find the perfect nanny for the little house.

Having Merry Perkins as a nanny would be a change, it was true. But it would be a good change. I was sure of it.

The Lemon Drops were singing "Jump Up and Dance." I jumped up and danced. I danced all around my room. I was feeling great.

L. GODWIN

About the Author

ANN M. MARTIN lives in New York City and loves animals, especially cats. She has two cats of her own, Gussie and Woody.

Other books by Ann M. Martin that you might enjoy are *Stage Fright*; *Me and Katie (the Pest)*; and the books in *The Baby-sitters Club* series.

Ann likes ice cream and *I Love Lucy*. And she has her own little sister, whose name is Jane.

Little Sister

Don't miss #106

KAREN'S PRESIDENT

"That is excellent," said Elizabeth. "I notice that your projects all have something in common. They would all benefit from a trip to Washington, D.C."

"Did you say *trip*?" I shouted.

"Indoor voice, please, Karen," said Elizabeth. "The answer is yes, I did say trip. The question is when."

"School will be closed in a week for winter vacation," said Kristy.

"That is right. The first weekend of vacation is right before Presidents' Day," I said.

"That sounds like the perfect time for a visit to the capital," said Daddy. "Has anyone made other plans yet?"

No one had made any other plans.

"Then I suggest we take a vote," said Daddy. "Whoever wants to go to Washington, D.C., say aye."

B·ABY·SITTERS ™

Little Sister

by Ann M. Martin
author of The Baby-sitters Club®

More Titles... ➡

PB
ER
Martin

The Baby-sitters Little Sister titles continued...

❑ MQ26301-3	#73	Karen's Dinosaur	$2.95
❑ MQ26214-9	#74	Karen's Softball Mystery	$2.95
❑ MQ69183-X	#75	Karen's County Fair	$2.95
❑ MQ69184-8	#76	Karen's Magic Garden	$2.95
❑ MQ69185-6	#77	Karen's School Surprise	$2.99
❑ MQ69186-4	#78	Karen's Half Birthday	$2.99
❑ MQ69187-2	#79	Karen's Big Fight	$2.99
❑ MQ69188-0	#80	Karen's Christmas Tree	$2.99
❑ MQ69189-9	#81	Karen's Accident	$2.99
❑ MQ69190-2	#82	Karen's Secret Valentine	$3.50
❑ MQ69191-0	#83	Karen's Bunny	$3.50
❑ MQ69192-9	#84	Karen's Big Job	$3.50
❑ MQ69193-7	#85	Karen's Treasure	$3.50
❑ MQ69194-5	#86	Karen's Telephone Trouble	$3.50
❑ MQ06585-8	#87	Karen's Pony Camp	$3.50
❑ MQ06586-6	#88	Karen's Puppet Show	$3.50
❑ MQ06587-4	#89	Karen's Unicorn	$3.50
❑ MQ06588-2	#90	Karen's Haunted House	$3.50
❑ MQ06589-0	#91	Karen's Pilgrim	$3.50
❑ MQ06590-4	#92	Karen's Sleigh Ride	$3.50
❑ MQ06591-2	#93	Karen's Cooking Contest	$3.50
❑ MQ06592-0	#94	Karen's Snow Princess	$3.50
❑ MQ06593-9	#95	Karen's Promise	$3.50
❑ MQ06594-7	#96	Karen's Big Move	$3.50
❑ MQ06595-5	#97	Karen's Paper Route	$3.50
❑ MQ06596-3	#98	Karen's Fishing Trip	$3.50
❑ MQ49760-X	#99	Karen's Big City Mystery	$3.50
❑ MQ50051-1	#100	Karen's Book	$3.50
❑ MQ50053-8	#101	Karen's Chain Letter	$3.50
❑ MQ50054-6	#102	Karen's Black Cat	$3.50
❑ MQ43647-3		Karen's Wish Super Special #1	$3.25
❑ MQ44834-X		Karen's Plane Trip Super Special #2	$3.25
❑ MQ44827-7		Karen's Mystery Super Special #3	$3.25
❑ MQ45644-X		Karen, Hannie, and Nancy The Three Musketeers Super Special #4	$2.95
❑ MQ45649-0		Karen's Baby Super Special #5	$3.50
❑ MQ46911-8		Karen's Campout Super Special #6	$3.25
❑ MQ55407-7		BSLS Jump Rope Pack	$5.99
❑ MQ73914-X		BSLS Playground Games Pack	$5.99
❑ MQ89735-7		BSLS Photo Scrapbook Book and Camera Pack	$9.99
❑ MQ47677-7		BSLS School Scrapbook	$2.95
❑ MQ13801-4		Baby-sitters Little Sister Laugh Pack	$6.99
❑ MQ26497-2		Karen's Summer Fill-In Book	$2.95

Available wherever you buy books, or use this order form.

Scholastic Inc., P.O. Box 7502, Jefferson City, MO 65102

Please send me the books I have checked above. I am enclosing $_____
(please add $2.00 to cover shipping and handling). Send check or money order – no
cash or C.O.Ds please.

Name_____ Birthdate_____

Address_____

City_____ State/Zip_____

Please allow four to six weeks for delivery. Offer good in U.S.A. only. Sorry, mail orders are not available to residents of Canada. Prices subject to change.   BSLS398